© 2023 Denny Hartmann
Drawings: Kimverly Faustino
Text: Denny Hartmann

For Tilda.

My one and only...

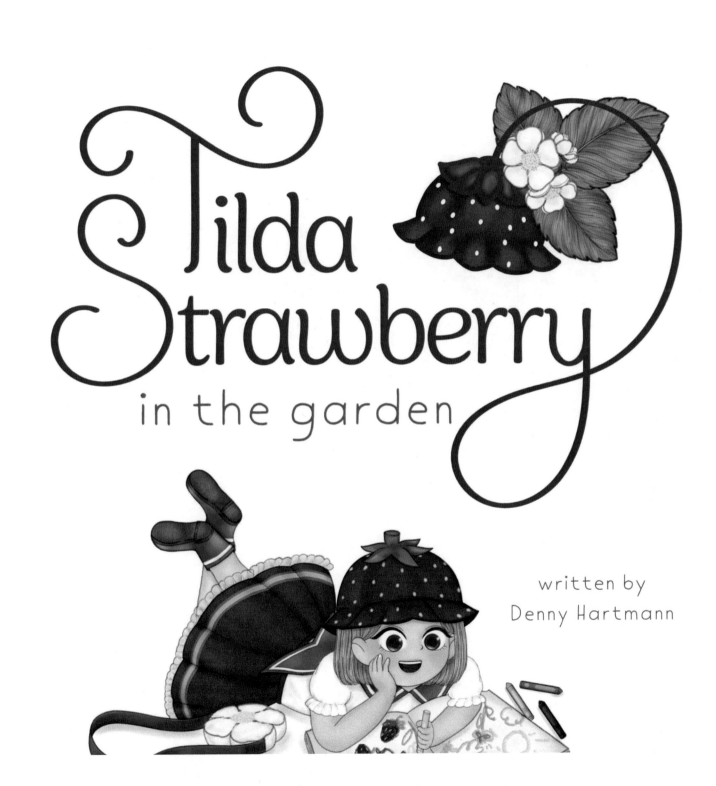

Tilda Strawberry
in the garden

written by
Denny Hartmann

Tilda woke up, looked at the mirror, smiled and sang, "I am beautiful, I am happy, this is a wonderful day la la la..."

Then Tilda smelled the fresh waffles that made her stomach ring like a bear cub's.
She hurried down the stairs.

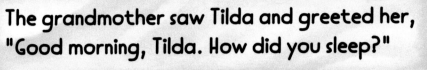

The grandmother saw Tilda and greeted her,
"Good morning, Tilda. How did you sleep?"

Tilda replied, "Good morning, Grandma. I slept well."
Grandma said, "That's good. Did you have a dream?"

Tilda sighed and replied, "Yes. I dreamed that I was spending the day with you and that we had something special planned, but then I woke up. What could that be, Grandma?"

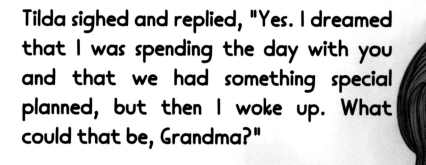

Grandmother replied, "I don't know. But I do know one thing: yes, we will spend time together today and do something special. We'll have to find out later. But for now, let's enjoy breakfast, okay?"

Tilda saw a smoothie on the table, and the moment she saw it, she was very thirsty.

Tilda nodded and agreed, "Okay, I'm looking forward to it. What kind of smoothie is this, Grandma?"
Grandma replied, "It's a strawberry smoothie."

Tilda sat down and could not wait to have a taste of the smoothie.
Tilda took a sip, and after a second, she reacted,
"This is yummy. Can I have strawberries, too?"

Grandma spoke, "Sure, Tilda. I'll get some for you."
Grandma took some strawberries from the
refrigerator and gave them to Tilda.

Tilda ate them with great pleasure. Grandma was very happy about it. "Thank you."

"Grandma, do you know that strawberries are my favorite fruit?" Grandma replied: "Yes, I can see that, my little angel. That's good that you like strawberries."

"Strawberries are very nutritious, and that's good for you. They're full of vitamins that help you stay healthy so you can do the things you like to do."

Tilda replied: "Wow, I'm going to eat even more strawberries from now on."

"Grandma, I have another question. Where do the strawberries and other fruit come from?" Grandma sat down and answered: "They come from gardens and farms. They are planted, tended and harvested when it's time to pick them."

Let's go into the garden, I want to show you something."
Tilda replied: "Oh yes, Grandma." Grandma went out through the back door. Tilda immediately got up and followed her.

Once in the garden, Tilda stopped and pointed to the ground, "Ew, a worm!"
Grandma replied, "That's an earthworm. Earthworms are very beneficial."
The earthworm disappeared into a hole in the ground.

Tilda replied: "Aren't earthworms harmful to plants?
Grandma replied: "No, my little angel, earthworms are not harmful. They are good for the soil and promote plant growth."
Tilda said: "That's good to know."

Now Tilda saw a butterfly.
Grandma said to Tilda: "And that's a butterfly."
Tilda asked: "What do butterflies do for plants, Grandma?"
Grandma said: "Butterflies help plants to produce seeds, like these strawberry seeds."
Tilda said, "Oh. The butterfly is pretty, just like me."

The grandmother said: "There's a bee here too."
The bee kept buzzing around.
Tilda asked: "Are bees good for plants too?"
The grandmother explained: "Without bees, the plants wouldn't bear fruit."
Then they both went into Grandma's greenhouse.

"And how do you plant strawberries now, Grandma?" asked Tilda.
Grandma took something out of a box and showed it to Tilda.
She said: "These are strawberry seeds. You have to plant them first so
that they can grow into a strawberry plant and take root."

"After a few days, we can see how they sprout and become seedlings, like here. Then you can plant them a few centimeters apart in their place in the garden and cover the roots with soil.

"Oh. I have a question. Our strawberries look very tasty already, Grandma. But how do strawberry plants grow?" asked Tilda.

Grandma replied: "You have to take good care of the strawberry plants, then they will grow."
"And how do you look after the plants, Grandma?"

Grandma fetched a watering can and poured water over a strawberry plant.

She replied: "I water them when they are dry. They also need sunlight to grow. And there's one more important thing."

Tilda was curious: "And what is that?"
Grandma leaned over and whispered, "I'm talking to them."
Tilda was surprised and asked, "Really, Grandma? What happens when you talk to them?"

Grandma replied with a grin: "They grow faster, my little angel."

Tilda put her hand over her mouth in amazement: "That's wonderful. Grandma, how long does a strawberry plant take to grow?"
"It takes about three months for them to bear fruit," replied her grandmother.

5 WEEKS

DAY   3 MONTHS   DAYS

"Four to six weeks after the plant has flowered, you can see the first strawberries. But they are still green and small. Then it takes a few more days until they get bigger and nice and red. Then you can pick them and they taste really good."
Tilda commented, "That's great, Grandma. It doesn't take that long at all."

"Did you know that there are over a hundred types of strawberries?" asked her grandmother. "There are big ones and small ones. But there are also white strawberries. They are also very tasty."

"Wow, there are so many of them, Grandma. I thought all strawberries were the same."

Grandma held Tilda's hand and they started to walk through the garden. She asked: "Would you like to help me pick dried leaves and harvest strawberries?" Tilda quickly replied: "Yes."

She was thrilled and felt good about helping Grandma. Tilda counted the strawberries she picked, one by one. And every now and then she ate one. When they had both finished, they put their baskets to one side.

Grandma pointed to the edge of the strawberry field: "Look, we have some seedlings here that can be planted. Do you want to plant them now, my little angel?

"Yes, I'd like to do that," Tilda replied. Grandma said, "I'll show you how to plant. Come with me."

The grandmother dug a hole with her hand shovel, planted a seedling and placed the roots in the hole. Then she covered the roots with soil.

Tilda followed her and asked after planting: "Did I do it right, Grandma?"
"Yes, you just need to put in a little more soil."
When the two of them had finished, they suddenly had 10 new strawberry plants.

Grandma praised Tilda: "Well done, my little angel. I'm proud of you. Your mom and dad will be proud of you too."

Tilda smiled and was happy. Tilda said: "Thank you, Grandma. It's fun being in the garden with you and helping you."

"I'm glad to hear that, Tilda. Next time I'll show you what else I can do in the garden.

Tilda smiled and replied: "I'm really looking forward to it. And what are we going to do with all the strawberries we've picked?"

Grandma replied, "We're going to do something special."
Tilda responded: "Something special? What is it, Grandma? Please tell me!"

Grandma grinned and said: "We're going to bake a big strawberry cake."

"Oh yes, Grandma, that's great.

While Tilda drew in her book, Grandma stirred the batter for the cake.

Tilda took a bite and replied: "It tastes so good. I had a lot of fun with you today. Thank you so much, Grandma."

Tilda hugged her grandma.